WORDS OF HOPE
— AND —
RESTORATION
of GOD

MR. PRESLEY WRIGHT

ISBN: 978-1-63950-232-5 (sc)
ISBN: 978-1-63950-233-2 (e)

This publication contains the opinions and ideas of its author. It is intended to provide helpful and informative material on the subjects addressed in the publication. The author and publisher specifically disclaim all responsibility for any liability, loss, or risk, personal or otherwise, which is incurred as a consequence, directly or indirectly, of the use and application of any of the contents of this book.

Writers Apex

Gateway Towards Success

8063 MADISON AVE #1252
Indianapolis, IN 46227
+13176596889
www.writersapex.com

www.cacbethel.com
www.igoeministry.com

CONTENTS

1. Hope is in Me, Jesus 1

2. God's Dreams and Your Life.. 2

3. God is Smiling are You 3

4. The Words I Speak From My Heart 4

5. The Love of God Never Fails.. 6

6. The Mirror that Reflects on Me 7

7. Stand Strong God is in Charge 8

8. The Holy Bible God Gave Me 9

9. Always Pray and Never Give Up 11

10. Miracles Just For You.. 12

11. Don't GIVE UP.. 13

12. It's Not About Us.. 14

13. Rejoice in the Lord Always...15

14. I Am The Great I Am 16

15. Don't Steal My Joy/God Gave You Some, Too 17

16. The Past is Your Sign Leave it Behind........................... 18

17. Do You Love Me? 19

18. It's a New Day 20

19. Help Me, Lord I Am Hurting.. 22

20. Lord, I Need Your Helping Hands.................................. 23

21. Pray for God's Guiding Hand 24

22. A Prayer for God's unspeakable Joy and Strength 25

23. Just One Touch of God's Love 26

24. Let Jesus Take the Wheel.. 27

Keep on Praying and Never Stop 36

I Believe in Miracles 37

Soldiers in the Army Of Lord 38

It's Not About Us 39

Rejoice in the Lord Always 40

I Am The Lord Your God 41

Don't Steal My Joy/ God Gave You Some Too 42

The Past Is Your Sign Leave It Behind 43

1

HOPE IS IN ME, JESUS

When I am in need, my **HOPE** is always there for me. It does not matter what time of day it may be—morning, noon, or midnight hour. My **HOPE** will be there for me. When I am hungry, **HOPE** prepares a table before me and gives me food to eat. He satisfies me and helps me to grow strong. When I'm thirsty, **HOPE** is there to provide me with water to drink to quench my thirst when I am hurt. When I am naked, **HOPE** will clothe me, hold me close to his heart, and wrap his loving arms around me. He(**JESUS**) said I love you more than you can ever imagine. Do you know that my love is true? My love won't hurt or reverse; I am always the same and never change. When I am in trouble, **HOPE** is always on time. When it was dark and I could not see, many obstacles were trying to block me. **HOPE** stood firm for me and brought me his light so I could see. When I was lonely and in despair, and no one else cared about me, Hope gave me his love, and he never left me. **HOPE** is right beside me when I smile, walk, or talk. When I don't know what direction to take, **HOPE** guides me and never leads me astray. It does not matter if I am in another city, country, or state; **HOPE** will always be there with me when I don't understand. **HOPE** is there to give me peace and hold me tight so I can sleep at night. When I am sick, **HOPE** will heal my body, make me whole, and provide me with life in my soul. Whether I am poor or rich, **HOPE** is there to take good care of me. Hope is more precious than the finest rubies, silver, and gold. Hope is for you and me. We all need Hope. When everything has failed all around me, my **HOPE** will always be deep in my heart and soul because he owns the throne. **Scripture: (Romans 5:3-5)** NIV- Not only so, but we also glory in our suffering because we know that suffering produces perseverance; perseverance, character, and character hope. And hope does not put us to shame, because God's love has been poured out into our hearts through the Holy Spirit, who has been given to us.

GOD'S DREAMS AND YOUR LIFE

Don't let your dreams slip away. Carry them with you daily; do not let them disappear because they can become a reality only if we continue praying. These dreams that we have seen are sometimes complicated for some to believe. We must keep them in our hearts deep down within. We must add the ingredients to these extraordinary dreams to become a reality. Add 3 cups of **LOVE,** 3 cups of **JOY,** and one mustard seed of **FAITH,** think positive every day, and stir all these unique ingredients together, and your dreams will become a reality. Keep the **FAITH** burning deep down within. Keep **HOPE** alive and **GOD'S LOVE** in your heart, and your dreams will become a reality.

Scripture: (Psalm 20:4)NIV- Grant thee according to thine own heart, and fulfill all thy counsel.

Scripture: (Jeremiah 29:11)NIV- For I know the thoughts that I think toward you saith the Lord, thoughts of peace, and not of evil, to give you an expected end.

3

GOD IS SMILING ARE YOU

I sat down by the blue ocean and the raging sea. I was sad about something and didn't understand what was wrong with me. I know God will help me. I looked down into the water and saw a reflection of me. I asked myself why I was not smiling on the beautiful day God created for me to see. As the wind blew, I reached out my hands to touch it, but I didn't know what direction it was blowing toward me as the waves flowed back and forth and crashed into the sea. I told myself that God has made amazing things for me to see. I looked up, and I was excited to see the birds of the air that flew by me. I looked to my right and left, and I heard the most beautiful sounds of the birds chirping toward me. Then I looked across the blue ocean, and birds started to land in the trees. I saw bluebirds, red birds, robin birds, sparrows, and all kinds of beautiful birds begin to surround me. They started to sing a song to me.

I did not understand what was going on. It's like God has sent them to me. I started to smile, and God said it's not hard to smile If you try, but it is easy to be sad as I bow down on my knees to pray to God. I told God about my day; he took my burdens and pains away. As you can see, he said (God) I am in control of everything, including the smile I gave you. So you can smile for me.

Scripture: (Job 9-27)NIV- If I say I will forget my complaint, I will change my expression, and smile; (Proverbs 15:13)NIV- A happy heart makes the face cheerful, but heartache crushes the spirit.

THE WORDS I SPEAK FROM MY HEART

As the sunrises from the deep blue sea, a beautiful day begins for me to see. On this day that God has granted unto me. I prayed to my Father God to ask him to forgive me. If I have a problem with the words that come out of my mouth from my heart, please help me stop. So, I must be careful of the words from my heart deep down within me. They are mighty. The words that I say come from my heart. I feel such great power deep down inside me when I speak these words that come to me; it gives me the power to my tongue, and my words reflect on me. The words that I speak from my heart, good or bad. They can create something powerful or give me Victory, sorrow, or shame. The words I speak carry a heavy weight. They can make me very strong or very weak. (God) I have uniquely created you with a special gift to say words that give you power, and victory is the kind of love that comes from my heart deep down inside me. I have given you a choice to speak life or death. It is now up to you to choose the right one. I have set you free, and now (Jesus Christ) has the keys, and I am well pleased. Your words are powerful.

As you can see, they come from your heart and mind deep down within. Words through prayer are the best way you could reach me. Words of love and forgiveness, to share your love for one another.

Sweet Savior named Jesus, who gave his whole heart. He expressed his love on the cross. Just remember one thing. Speaking positive words gives life to our souls, and negative words are like feeding poison to our minds, which breaks my heart. So, you must be careful of the words you speak out of your mouth that come from your heart.

Scripture: NIV- (Proverbs 18:21) Death and life are in the power of the tongue, and they that love it shall eat the fruit thereof.

Scripture: NIV- (Matthew 15: 18) But those things which proceed out of the mouth come forth from the heart; they defile a man.

5

THE LOVE OF GOD NEVER FAILS

My love for you comes from my heart in many unique ways you never knew. Here are a few ways to express a special love I created for you. I never fail to give you two legs, hands, and two feet that are so unique. I have also given you strength and power for all these parts, even a mouth to talk. I never fail to give you a loving heart from the start. My love is true even when you feel blue. Listen to the rhythm. Do you hear the beating every time it beats? It tells how deep my love is for you. I never fail to give you two beautiful eyes that are so pure and bright so you can see the most beautiful thing all around you that I have created for you and me to see. I never fail to give you two ears to hear. When you listened to my voice, you ran to me, sat down, paid close attention, and listened. I whisper to them softly, come close to me, don't be afraid. I love you; I want to tell you how much I care and let you know I will always be there. I never fail to give you two hands to touch and hold my unchanging hand and to feel my special love for you. I never fail to give you a tongue to speak to the highest mountain in the sea. To remove those obstacles blocking you. I never fail to breathe life into you. Made you whole and gave you life to your soul. I give you hope and faith deep down within your soul so that you can believe what I can do for you. You have never seen it before. I am the Creator of the Creation, as you can see. I have created you to be a Masterpiece that you never knew. I have plans for you and will never harm you. I love you very much. I will never leave you or forsake you.

Scripture: (Psalms 94:18-19)NIV- When I said, "My foot is slipping," your unfailing love, Lord, supported me. When anxiety was great within me, your consolation brought me joy.

6

THE MIRROR THAT REFLECTS ON ME

The mirror that reflects on me has a significant impact on me. It is life or death, however, it may appear to me. So when I face this mirror that reflects on me, it is who I am, my character, and my weight. It is what I do and how I act accordingly. I must be careful with my words because they could destroy or help me. Speaking life soothes the heart and eases the soul. I see good things happening to me and life more abundantly. As I face the mirror that significantly affects me, good or bad, it is up to me. I said to myself; I want to please God, not myself. I started praying to my God, who has done marvelous things for me. God speaks to me: you have a choice. It is entirely up to you. I have set you free. Now I can see clearly. A brighter and lighter reflection of me when God showed me I have the victory. I know God has great plans for me.

Scripture: (1 Corinthians 13:12)NIV- For now we see only a reflection as in a mirror; then we shall see face to face. Now I know in part; then I shall know fully, even as I am fully known.

7

STAND STRONG GOD IS IN CHARGE

Together, we stand divided, we fall. No Prayer, we fall; with Prayer, we conquer all. Stand on my word. I cannot lie; you will never lose. I will be right beside you; I am always on time. No Hope we fall; with Hope, we stand on the promises of God. No Faith, we fall; with Faith, we stand. We walk and put on the whole Armor Of God. No Love, we fall; with Love, we stand in Honor with the Love of Jesus Christ in our hearts who conquer it all. No Peace, we fall; with Peace, we give it to God, who understands it all. We will stand with Victory and the Power to stand firm for God. Divided, we fall, and the enemy (devil) will come to steal, kill, and destroy. Just remember I am your God, and nothing will ever defeat you. You will never fight this battle alone. I am in complete control; just remember, stand strong for me. I am in charge. I am your God.

Scripture: (Ephesians 6: 10,13-14) Finally, my brethren, be strong in the Lord and in the power of his might. Wherefore take unto you the whole armor of God, that ye may be able to withstand in the evil day, and having done all, to stand. Stand, therefore, having your loins girt about with truth, and having on the breastplate of righteousness.

8

THE HOLY BIBLE GOD GAVE ME

The Holy Bible God gave me is a mystery that cannot be solved. Because no one can figure out the things of Almighty God, it's my life when **HE** breathes his **RESURRECTION SPIRIT** inside me on the earth and death for **ETERNITY**. It encourages me to stand on God's word, trust him, and always be strong. The Holy Bible God gave me is magnificent, a sharp sword that cuts deep, Supernatural, and very powerful, as you can see. The Holy Bible God gave me is so good, fruitful, and sweet as the honey in the honeycomb. As I travel this long road, I may not know what's ahead of me. The Holy Bible that God gave me is my road map. I can always look up to Him because He is my **KING,** and **HE** is on the **THORNE**. I have to follow him (God) and do things **HIS WAY**, not my own. I must continue to obey, submit myself to God, and always pray. Surrender to him, worship and praise, love him, and follow **HIS TEN COMMANDMENTS**. The Holy Bible God gave me is part of my body in many ways. His powerful words exploded inside of me. The Holy Bible God gave me is my future and everything I need to know. The Holy Bible gives me guidance, correction, love, and affection. The Holy Bible God Gave me is incredible and has so much to explain; you must taste it to see for yourself, and you will say the same. The Holy Bible God has given me has a special place: my heart and soul. I know I already have the victory. The Holy Bible God gave me has so many benefits to offer me. The Holy Bible God gave me peace, Victory, joy, and hope. I'm not going to stop there; let me tell you more. It gives me peace that passes all my understanding. It gives me hope that I know his promises are for sure. It gives me victory that I can see and has already defeated my worst (devil) enemy. I would like to say something else about my Holy Bible. As I continue to pray, my God will show me the way. The

Holy Bible God gave me does not hate, criticize, persecute, or lie. Now I know who I will always follow and obey. My God and the Holy Bible God gave me. He will never lead me the wrong way because he loves me, providing me peace and knowing he will always be beside me.

Scripture: (Isaiah 41:10-)" Don't fear because I am with you; don't be afraid, for I am your God. I will strengthen you, I will surely help you; I will hold you with my righteous strong hand."

9

ALWAYS PRAY AND NEVER GIVE UP

When things are going well, pray?

When things are not the way you think they should be, pray?

When you don't understand why things happen this way, pray?

When things don't go your way, pray?

When you don't understand why people get hurt in so many ways, pray?

When there is pain in your body, pray?

When we don't understand why some will love you from their hearts, some will love you in their way, pray?

When you don't understand why there is so much pain, pray.

Just remember one thing: our way is not God's way.

His ways are remarkable in every way.

So, let God have his way! Prayer is one of our most powerful weapons to fight against our worst enemy.

As for me, you let us continue to pray and put all our heart, soul, and hope in our God because he is our bright and morning star. So, Prayer is the answer! Faith opens the door. Hope is all you need, and it will help you grow.

Scripture: (Isaiah 55:8) For my thoughts are not your thoughts, neither are your ways my ways, says the Lord.

MIRACLES JUST FOR YOU

I believe in God; I believe in Miracles too!

I believe in signs and wonders only God can perform for you.

I believe in the healing hands, and the delivering power only God can do for you.

I trust him with all my heart because he has loved me from the very start.

I know I can do all things through Christ, who has strengthened me because

God can work a Miracle through you and me.

I am a part of the body of Christ; as you can see, that is why God has Miracles for you and me!

Scripture: (Deuteronomy 10:21) He is the one you praise; he is your God, who perform for you those great and awesome wonders you saw with your own eyes."

11

DON'T GIVE UP

Keep going. Soldiers keep marching!

Lord, I can't see! The enemy threw some dirt into my eyes and blinded me. I am your sight when you can not see. Your enemy under your feet. Now you have the victory. I will guide you along the way. Keep going, Soldiers, keep marching! Lord, I can't walk! We walk by faith and not by sight. I will be right beside you when you walk. Lord, I can't speak! I will talk to you and give you the words to say. Do not be afraid. I am with you always, and I will never leave you alone. Lord, I can't stand on my own! I will give you strength to stand; just hold on, my child. I will always be there for you, never leave you, and always care for you, so don't give up on me, and I will never give up on you. That is the promise I made to you.

Scripture: (Joshua 1:9) (NET) I repeat, be strong and brave! Don't be afraid and don't panic, for I the Lord your God, am with you in all you do."

IT'S NOT ABOUT US

It's not about me, and it's not about you. It's about Jesus. Sharing his love. In an extraordinary way on this beautiful day. It wouldn't take much, but it can tremendously change someone's life in a big way. It could be a hug, a smile, a handshake, a simple hello, a kiss on the cheek, and tell them how much you love them while they are here and near.

Think about this for a moment. It was love that lifted you and me. It was His grace and mercy that brought us through. God cares about us. Do we care about one another because he (Jesus) shared his life when he died on the cross for you and me?

Scripture: (John 13:34-35) A new commandment I give unto you, that ye love one another, as I have loved you, that ye also love one another. By this shall all men know that ye are my disciple if ye have love one to another.

13

REJOICE IN THE LORD ALWAYS

Know God, feel God, feel good. I know it's hard sometimes when we are going through trials in our lives. The enemy(devil) wants us to feel sad, mad, stressed, depressed, and blue. Always remember God loves you very much! When you are going through a trial. God knows what to do when you are feeling blue. He will always be there for you! He loves you more than you will ever know because he cares for you. God wants you to be happy, joyful, and glad. Not sad, mad, and blue. He is in control of all things, and that includes you too. So don't worry, he will always love you.

Scripture: (Psalm 32:11) Be glad in the Lord, rejoice ye righteous: shout for joy, all ye that are upright in heart.

14

I AM THE GREAT I AM

I am always here for you. I am here when you are going through a storm. I am the I am; I will be there for you. I will protect you, shield you so that nothing will harm you, my child. When the lightning strikes, I will stretch out my hands to save you. I am the I am. I will guide you when the thunder roars and tell you what to do. I will always be there for you. I am, I am. I love you when no one else cares about you, but I do, and when you thought you were alone and on your own. I was always there to take care of you. I am the I am. I am here for you when you have lost a loved one so close to your heart, dear to you. I understand. I will be beside you and comfort you in your time of need. I am the I am. I have shared so many things with you, including my love for you, from my heart that you never knew. I will always be there for you. I am the I am. I am hope when you thought it was the end for you. I am the I am. I am joy when you are sad, lonely, and in despair. I will be there for you. I am the I am. I am peace that passes all understanding when you try to figure things out independently and don't know what to do. I will take care of you. I am the I am. I will rest your mind and soul and make you whole. Let me fight this battle for you. It does not belong to you, and you don't know what to do. I am the I am. I am your sunshine on a gloomy and cloudy day; don't be sad. I will brighten up all things for you. I am the I am. So smile, and always know in your heart and your soul. I will always be there for you.

Scripture: (Psalm 46:10) Be still and know that I am God I will be exalted among the heathen, I will be exalted in the earth.

Scripture: (Isaiah 41:10) Fear thou not; I am with thee: be not dismayed; for I am thy God: I will strengthen thee; yea, I will help thee; yea I will uphold thee with my right hand of my righteousness.

15

DON'T STEAL MY JOY/
GOD GAVE YOU SOME, TOO

As you rose out of your bed on a new day, God gave you. You should be joyful that God has spared your life and made you brand new. Don't steal my joy; God gave you some, too. As you look up to the beautiful sky that God has made for me and you to see, look at the different shapes, colors, sun, birds, beautiful flowers, and green trees. Don't steal my joy; God gave you some, too. God is in control of your life in all that you do. He wants you to smile, be happy, not sad and blue, and enjoy every moment while God has given you life on this brand-new day you never knew. Don't steal my joy; God gave you some, too. Enjoy life to the fullest, sit by the blue ocean, and enjoy the view as the waves flow back and forth to you. Don't steal my joy; God gave you some, too. When others feel blue, cheer them up, and God will reward you. He loves us so much more than we ever knew. He gave us joy that will take sorrows and pain away, and there will be no more. So don't steal my joy; God gave you some, too.

Scripture: (John 15:11) These things that I have spoken unto you, that my joy might remain in you, and your joy might be full.

Scripture: (John 16:22) And now, therefore, have sorrow: but I will see you again, and your heart shall rejoice, and your joy no man taketh from you.

16

THE PAST IS YOUR SIGN LEAVE IT BEHIND

It does not matter what you are going through. Whatever problems you may have, significant or minor, leave the past behind you. God knows what to do for you; he cares and will always be there. Leave it there and put it in God's hand. He understands he has a plan: walk up boldly with your head high up to the sky and don't be shy. God knows all about your hurts, pains, and sorrows. You would say to myself that no one understands me, and God would say back to you I do, which is why I love you. The future is near you, so stop looking back at your past when you don't know what to do. It is very bright as the faith that is in you. Let the God of this universe take control of your life; he knows what to do and come to Jesus. He will make everything all right for you. Put your trust in him. He will teach you and show you the way as you pray. Just remember, God sits up high and looks down below. God knows about your troubles, sorrows, and pain. Leave the past behind you.

Scripture: (Philippians 3:13-14) Brothern, I count not myself to have apprehended: but this one thing I do, forgetting those things which are behind, and reaching forth unto those things which are before, I press toward the mark for the prize of the high calling of God in Christ Jesus.

DO YOU LOVE ME?

Do you love me for who I am? Do you love me as you say you do? Think about this for a moment. Do you love me because of my skin color, nationality, or maybe the state I'm in? Do you mean it deep down within? Do you love me as you say you do? The heart may say what shall I do, but the mind may wonder what to do. Do you love me if I could walk or stand.? Do you love me if I am hungry or thirsty? Maybe I need a helping hand? Do you love me as you say you do? Do you love me if I am big, small, tall, or short? Do you love me if I am smart or not? Do you love me if I am in the hospital or at home? I may be a stranger to you; do love as you say you do. Would you please help me and take me by my hand? Do you love me? Do you love me if I wear raggedy clothes and no shoes or socks? Do you love me? If I had hair on my head or bald on the top? Do you love me rather than if I am rich or poor and have nowhere to go? Do you love me if I smile or not? Do you love as you say you do? Do you love me if I eat out of a trash can and you eat at a table? Do you care enough to say hello? I will say back to you with a smile. Talk to you soon. (God) when all kinds of love have failed around you, you can depend on me to bring you through. I love you more than you ever knew. I love you when no one understands what you are going through. It doesn't matter what condition or shape you are in. I will always be there with you until the very end.

Scripture: (NIV)1 Corinthians 13:4-8 Love is patient, love is kind. It does not envy, it does not boast, it is not proud. It is not rude, it is not self-seeking, it is not easily angered, it keeps no record of wrongs. Love does not delight in evil but rejoices with the truth.

Scripture: (John 15:12) This is my commandment, That ye love one another, as I have loved you.

18

IT'S A NEW DAY

It's a new day upon the land we have **Faith** in our **God**, and now we can stand on his word, for it is true because this is the day the Lord has made for you and me. Rejoice, rejoice. It is a blessing to praise His **Holy** name. It is a new day of **Peace**. Whatever problem you may have put in the **Master's Hand**. Always keep in mind that our **God** has the **Best Plan.** It's a new day of **Hope**; just look around at the beautiful, lovely things **God** has made for you and me. Look at the beautiful trees, the roses, and all the other flowers that make it so complete. Look up, and you will see the sun that glows down on you and me. When we were walking in darkness, but now we could see. It is the most beautiful light, radiant as it can be. It is a new day to go out and possess the lands, plow the fields, and plant our seeds in good grounds. Sit down at the table and enjoy the goodness of the Lord because the enemy is under our feet. Now, we can eat and celebrate the **Harvest** that **God** has prepared for you and me. It's a new day to relax. Our **God** is in control. Sit by the water And look around the ocean in the deep blue sea. It's a new day. It's not a day of sadness but a day of gladness. Look at the boys, girls, squirrels, and birds in the trees. Look at the blue skies and the beautiful colors, forms, and shapes God created for me and you. It's a new day to lift your hands, rise, and pray to the **Highest God, Mighty and Powerful, who** made everything. It's a new day to open your mouth, stand up on your feet, and give **God** all the **praise.** He's in control of this beautiful day that he has made. It's a new day to say **God** has done many amazing things for me. **God** is good all the time, and he never fails. Let us celebrate! It is a new day! **God** has given us so much grace. Throw the confetti to the **Bridegroom (Jesus)** and the **Bride (Church). Let** us celebrate; it is a new day. Let go of all the balloons, as beautiful as they can be. There are so many different colors and shapes, as you can see. Out of your hands, set them free! Into the atmosphere and let the breeze of the winds expand their air. They will soon fade away, and you won't be able to see them anymore. As we look up excitedly, we breathe, inhale, and exhale because Jesus has set us free. Let's celebrate, celebrate **God** is good. It's a new day to bring out Shofar, Tambourines, Cymbals, Bells, Reed-Pipe, Lyre, Harp, Flutes, and Voices. Let's make a joyful noise unto the Lord, give our God all the praises, and sing a **new song** to our **God** because it is a new day.

Scripture: (Psalm 118:23-24) (GNT) 23 This was done by the LORD; what a wonderful sight it is! 24 This is the day of the LORD's victory; let us be happy, let us celebrate!

19

HELP ME, LORD I AM HURTING

I'm hurting, **LORD,** Deep down in my heart and the core of my soul. I don't know what to do. Please, Lord, give me the strength to stand, take me by my hand, and help me get through. **LORD,** I know you will provide me with the time to explain. Here we go all over again, as the teardrops roll down, my face so ashamed. It is hard to understand as the storm rages in my life and the wind blows behind my back, but I trust your plans. As the dark clouds roll away and the sun rises the next day.

You are my **SHEPHERD.** I am your sheep. You are the only one who can guide me through this old valley of darkness and shame. Only you, Lord, can move these rugged stains, the hurt, and the pain. I know you will never leave me alone or forsake me; you will always be there for me. My blessings are on the way. **(LORD) I AM** the **LORD** thy **GOD,** and **I AM** in control of the storms of the air and the raging wind against your back. You have nothing to fear. **I AM** here through the darkest moments of your life. I will lighten up your path. I will be there when you're in the deepest valley down beneath. Are on the highest mountain upon the sea. I will be beside you to dry all your tears and move all your fears. Just put all your trust in me. **I AM** your **SHEPHERD,** and you are my sheep. Who I will always take good care of and who will always be near.

Scripture: (NIV) (Isaiah 41:10) So do not fear, for I am with you; do not be dismayed, for I am your God. I will strengthen you and help you; I will uphold you with my right hand. (Rev.21:4) He will wipe every tear from their eyes. There will be no more death or mourning or crying or pain, for the old order of things has passed away."

20

LORD, I NEED YOUR HELPING HANDS

I look toward heaven; all of my help comes from you because you sit up high on the throne, and you already know there are things I must go through in my life. **FAITH-** Give me the faith I need to keep my eyes on you. I know I can always depend on you, in Jesus' name. Because you are always the same and you will never change. I give up. I give it all to you, Lord. My heart and my soul belong to you. I put all of my trust in you. I will always keep my hands in your unchanging hands. Now I can walk up straight to you and always follow you. **Hope-** Give me hope when all is lost, even when I come crying to you. It may challenge my faith as I continue to walk with you. But I do not doubt you.

Even when I am weak, and you are strong. But I will always trust you because your promises are golden, as I am encouraged and wait patiently for you. **Courage-** Give me the courage to be strong like a roaring lion. To have no fear in my heart and deep down in the depths of my soul, and give this battle I am fighting to you. **Peace-**Give me peace when I am confused as you fight this battle, and I do not know what to do. I may not understand what is happening, but I know you do. I will always put all my trust in you. **Joy-** Give me joy when I am sad, depressed, and stressed. Give me the strength that I need to endure. **Love -** You give me the love I need when wounded, hurting and bleeding. I know you will not turn your back on me when no one else cares about me, and I know you always do.

Scripture: Psalms 121 1-2 (NIV) I lift up my eyes to the mountain where does my help comes from? 2- My help comes from the Lord, the Maker of heaven and earth. Psalms 146 (NIV) 5- Blessed are those whose help is the God of Jacob, whose hope is in the Lord their God. (NIV) Isaiah 41:10 So do not fear, for I am with you; do not be this dismayed, for I am your God. I will strengthen you and help you; I will uphold you with my righteous right hand.

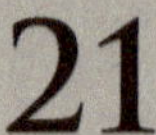

21

PRAY FOR GOD'S GUIDING HAND

Heavenly Father, my Guiding friend, light and shining star that shines so bright, powerful, and Almighty Wonderful Counselor Powerful God. Who made Heaven and Earth? I come boldly to you in my weakest state from my heart and my mind to the throne of your Grace. I need your direction and your correction. I do not know what to do, and I need your Guidance. Have mercy on me, Lord, and show me your way. I follow your footsteps, obey your commands, and hear your spirit's quiet, still voice as you lead the way. I give you all the praise. Teach me, Lord, your ways, and order my steps in your word. Take me by my hand, and I will follow you. Because you are the King of Kings and sit up high and looks down low because you own the throne of grace; and look upon me daily. Help me, Heavenly Father, make the right decisions as I continue to pray unto you. I have made so many wrong decisions, and I have learned a valuable lesson along the way. Heavenly Father, give me the faith to stand, courage, and move all fear from inside of me. I am depending on you to carry me on and be strong. I will trust you as I walk, run, or stop to look both ways. Direct my paths and lead me in the path of your righteousness for your name's sake. I know you have extraordinary plans for me, and you will not harm me in any way. I will always wait for you to guide me daily.

IN JESUS NAME AMEN

A PRAYER FOR GOD'S UNSPEAKABLE JOY AND STRENGTH

Loving Father, King of All Kings, and the ruler of the nations. Who has given us so much more than we ever know or deserve? Your unspeakable Joy and strength. Where there is no shame, whom all blessing flows in the deepest of the deep rivers and the depth of my soul, you are the Lord of Lords, the creator of my life, and the owner of my dying soul. You are the peacemaker of peace that will not harm my crying soul. I thank you for your strength because I am weary and weak in my bones; only you can help me stand firm. Lord, I ask you to give me the courage to stand on your word and faith because I know you will never leave me alone. With my eyes lifted, all my attention is only on you. To my understanding, my heart belongs to you. You are the giver of my life and receiver of all blessings, wonderful counselor, and heaven treasures that belong to you. Let the walls of my life. Be Filled with your precious Holy Spirit from above and your unconditional love in me. Fill every word of sadness with your unspeakable joy and strength to every bone. So I will be able to stand and be strong. Then, Lord, take me by my hands, lift me up, and place my feet in your hands until my journey in this world is complete.

IN JESUS NAME AMEN

JUST ONE TOUCH OF GOD'S LOVE

Heaven Father, You are everything I need. I can not live without you. You are the God of many nations, a strong and mighty peacemaker, a Miracle Worker who can do the impossible for those who believe in you. Ruler of all people. Owner and foundation of my body, mind, and soul. I surrender all to you. Thank you for all the doctors, nurses, and those you have used as I go through this season of sickness, but I put all my faith and trust only in you. You are my healer; nothing can compare to you. You are the Healer of all diseases. Let there be no sickness, pain, or suffering that I can not overcome. Always be active in my mind, body, and soul; serve you; and let your will, purpose, and plan be done with your love, faith, and courage to be strong in you and confident to always depend on you. Keep me close to your heart, comfort me in my time of need, and give me the patience to wait on you. From the morning when I rise up and at night when I lay down my head.

IN JESUS NAME AMEN!

24

LET JESUS TAKE THE WHEEL

Let Jesus take the wheel! Whatever road you travel on this lovely day, give him your life today. Listen! Let Jesus take the wheel; let it go. He is in control; give it to him, and you worry no more. But there is only one road that we must stay focused on. The straight and narrow way that will lead you to saving grace. Let Jesus take the wheel, stop fighting, and let it go; he will teach you along the way. We can't solve these problems on our own. Jesus has the answer, and he will make a way. We travel many types of roads every day, but let him take control and have his way. Pay attention, stay focused, and keep your eyes on the road. Because something, anything, or anyone can come across your pathway, and you may not know. When we try to figure things out on our own, we always come up a little short, and in our minds, we think we are constantly correct but wrong. Listen! Let Jesus take the wheel. You can not figure it out. Let Jesus lead you to his throne, where you will find his loving grace. Because he loves you so much, he does not want you to go the wrong way. When you thought you were all alone. He is right beside you. Let Jesus take the wheel. Some roads are pitch dark, and it is impossible to see anything at all. Now, you are lost, where no light is in sight. You would say to yourself what shall I do? Listen! Let Jesus take the wheel. Let it go! He is the Way, the Truth, and the Light. He will make everything bright! Because he is the bright morning star that comprehends the darkest road in your life. Listen! Let Jesus take the wheel. Some roads are smooth, and others can be rough and short. These roads can be very challenging to our faith. But they are part of our lives, and we may not understand what is happening. We may be afraid, but we must take them anyway. Listen! Let Jesus take the wheel! Let it go! Just sit back, breathe in, and breathe out, relax. Listen, can you hear that quiet, still voice? Let me drive and lead the way. Just be still and know that I am God. The rocky road. And the dirt road. These roads can cause you to lose traction, which is very hard to control. When we do not have control, listen! Let it go, and let Jesus lead the way. Let Jesus take the wheel in your life today. The intersection road. This road may confuse you because it gives you many choices. The south, north, east, and the west. That can lead you to go in so many different directions. Listen! Let Jesus take the wheel! This road also has many types of traffic lights: red, yellow, and green, and many other warning signs around it. We must always be careful and open our eyes. Take heed, and don't be deceived, but always obey. Our lives can sometimes be very harsh, and we face many challenges. But let Jesus take the wheel of your life and give you Sufficient Grace. So, we must stay focused on the right road as we travel. But let Jesus drive and give him your life. Just let it go! Let Jesus take the wheel in your life today.

Scripture: (Psalm 32:8) I will instruct you and teach you in the way you should go; I will counsel you with my loving eye on you.

ABOUT THIS BOOK OF WORDS
OF HOPE AND RESTORATION OF GOD

The Words of Hope are in me and you that come through our heart and soul. Through the Love of Jesus Christ, our Lord and Savior. God's hands Created us, our Father in Heaven, the creator of all things on earth and in Heaven. He restores our souls and gives us a place to lay our heads. This book has stories, poems, and prayers. That is uplifting, inspirational, encouraging words. This book will give you hope through life experiences, trials, and tribulations.

GETTING TO KNOW THE AUTHOR:
MR.PRESLEY WRIGHT

Life for me was very challenging, but my faith in Jesus Christ. The evidence of my hope in him is to keep moving on and be strong. God gave me unconditional love through Jesus Christ, the king of Glory. Through many trials and tribulations. His love and Hope were always there to rescue me. I have found all my hope in Jesus Christ, my Savior. I put all my trust in him. He is the author and the finisher of my faith.

REFLECTION NOTES

REFLECTION NOTES

REFLECTION NOTES

REFLECTION NOTES

REFLECTION NOTES

REFLECTION NOTES

KEEP ON PRAYING AND NEVER STOP

When things are going good, pray?

When things are not the way you think they should be, pray?

When you don't understand why things happen this way, pray?

When things don't go your way, pray?

When you don't understand why people get hurt in so many ways, pray?

When there is pain in your body, pray?

When we don't understand why some will love you from their hearts, some will love you in their own way, and some will hate in so many ways pray?

When you don't understand, you say to yourself why are these things happening to me? God said I will show you the way just stay on your knees and always pray?

Just remember one thing our way is not God's way.

His ways are excellent in every way.

So let God have his way!

As for me, and you let us continue to pray and move out of his way. So prayer is the answer! Faith opens the door! Hope is what you need and God is the one who we adore.

Scripture: (Isaiah 55:8) For my thoughts are not your thoughts, neither are your ways my ways, says the Lord.

I BELIEVE IN MIRACLES

I believe in God, and I believe in Miracles too!

I believe in signs and wonders only God can perform for you.

I believe in the healing hands, and the delivering power only God can do for you.

I put my trust in him, with all my heart, because he loves me from the very start.

I know I can do all things through Christ who has strengthened me because,

God can work a Miracle through you and me.

I am a part of the body of Christ as you can see that is why God has Miracles for you and me!

Scripture: (Deuteronomy 10:21) He is the one you praise; he is your God, who perform for you those great and awesome wonders you saw with your own eyes"

SOLDIERS IN THE ARMY OF LORD

Keep going, soldiers keep marching!

Lord, I can't see! I am your sight when you can not see, I will guide you. Lord, I can't walk! We walk by faith, and not by sight, I will be right beside you when you walk. Lord, I can't speak! I will speak to you and give you the words to say. Be not afraid I am with you always, and I will never leave you alone. Lord, I can't stand on my own! I will give you the strength to stand, just hold on to my unchanging hand. I will always be there for you, I will never leave you, I will always care for you so don't give up on me, and I will never give up on you.

Scripture: Philippians 4:13 I can do all things through Christ which strengtheneth me.

IT'S NOT ABOUT US

It's not about me, and it's not about you. It's about Jesus sharing his love today. It won't take much, but it can tremendously change someone's life. It could be a hug, a smile, a handshake, a simple hello, a kiss on the cheek, and tell them how much you love them while they are here and near.

Think about this for a moment. It was his love that lifted me, and you. It was His grace and mercy that brought us through. God cares about us, do we care about one another, because he (Jesus) shared his life when he died on the cross for me, and you?

Scripture: John 13:34-35 A new commandment I give unto you, that ye love one another, as I have loved you, that ye also love one another. By this shall all men know that ye are my disciple if ye have love one to another.

REJOICE IN THE LORD ALWAYS

Know God, love God and feel good. I know it's hard sometimes when we are going through trials in our lives. The enemy(devil) wants us to feel sad, mad, stressed, depressed, and blue. Always remember God loves you very much! When you are going through a trial, God knows what to do when you are feeling blue. He will always be there for you! He loves you more than you will ever know because he cares for you. God wants you to be happy, joyful, and glad. Not sad, mad, and blue. He is in control of all things, and that includes you too. So don't worry he will always love you.

Scripture: Psalm 32:11 Be glad in the Lord, rejoice ye righteous: shout for joy, all ye that are upright in heart.

I AM THE LORD YOUR GOD

I am here always for you. I am here when you are going through a storm. I am the I am, I will be there for you. I will protect you, shield you so nothing will harm you, my child. When the lightning strikes I will stretch out my hands to you and save you. I am the I am. When the thunder roars I will guide you, and tell you what to do. I will always be there for you. I am I am. I am loved when no one else cares about you, but I do, and when you thought you were all alone and on your own. I was always there to take care of you. I am the I am. I am here for you when you have lost a loved one so close to heart, and dear to you. I understand. I will be right beside you and comfort you in your time of need. I am the I am. I have shared so many things with you, and that includes my love for you from my heart that you never knew. I will always be there for you. I am the I am. I am hope when you thought it was the end for you. I am the I am. I am joy when you are sad, lonely, and in despair. I will be there for you. I am the I am. I am peace that passes all understanding when you try to figure things out on your own, and you don't know what to do. I will take care of you. I am the I am. I will give you rest to your mind, and soul and make you whole. Let me fight this battle for you, it does not belong to you and you don't know what to do. I am the I am. I am your sunshine on a gloomy, and cloudy day don't be sad. I will brighten up all things for you. I am the I am. So smile, and always know in your heart, and your soul. I will always be there for you.

Scripture: Psalm 46:10 Be still and know that I am God I will be exalted among the heathen, I will be exalted in the earth. Isaiah 41:10 Fear thou not; I am with thee: be not dismayed; for I am thy God: I will strengthen thee; yea, I will help thee; yea I will uphold thee with my right hand of my righteousness.

DON'T STEAL MY JOY/ GOD GAVE YOU SOME TOO

As you rose out of your bed on a brand new day that God has given you. You should be happy that God has spared your life and made you brand new. Don't steal my joy God gave you some too. As you look up to the beautiful sky that God has made for me and you to see, look at the different shapes, colors, and the sun, the birds, the beautiful flowers, and the green trees. Don't steal my joy God gave you some too. God is in control of your life in all that you do. He wants you to smile, and be happy, not sad and blue, and enjoy every moment while God has given you life on this brand new day that you never knew. Don't steal my joy God gave you some too. To enjoy life to the fullest, sit down by the blue ocean, and enjoy the view as the waves flow back and forward to you. Don't steal my joy God gave you some too. When others feel blue, cheer them up, and help them along the way, God will reward you. He loves us so much more than we ever knew. He gave us joy that will take sorrows and pain away there will be no more. So don't steal my joy, God gave you some too.

Scripture: John 15:11 These things that I have spoken unto you, that my joy might remain in you, and your joy might be full. John 16:22 And now, therefore, have sorrow: but I will see you again, and your heart shall rejoice, and your joy no man taketh from you.

THE PAST IS YOUR SIGN
LEAVE IT BEHIND

It does not matter what you are going through. What problems you may have, big, or small, leave the past behind you. God knows what to do for you, he cares, and will always be there for you. Leave it there and put it in God's hands he understands he has a plan, walk boldly with your head high up to the sky, and don't be shy. God knows all about your hurts, pains, and sorrows. You would say to yourself that no one understands me, and God would say back to you I do, which is why I love you. Before you stop looking back at your past, the future is when you don't know what to do. Look up to your future. It is very bright as the faith that is in you. Let the God of this universe take control of your life, he knows what to do, and come to Jesus he will make everything all right for you. If you put your trust in him. He will teach you, and show you the way, as you continue to pray. Just remember he sits up high and looks down below, he knows about your troubles, he knows about your sorrows and your pains. Give it to God, he loves you, he is always the same. So leave the past behind you.

Scripture: Philippians 3:13-14 Brethren, I count not myself to have apprehended: but this one thing I do, forgetting those things which are behind, and reaching forth unto those things which are before, 14 I press toward the mark for the prize of the high calling of God in Christ Jesus.